T0246324

At first it was just a nasty nip on a little girl's finger. But soon the bite from her new pet turned into something much more serious.

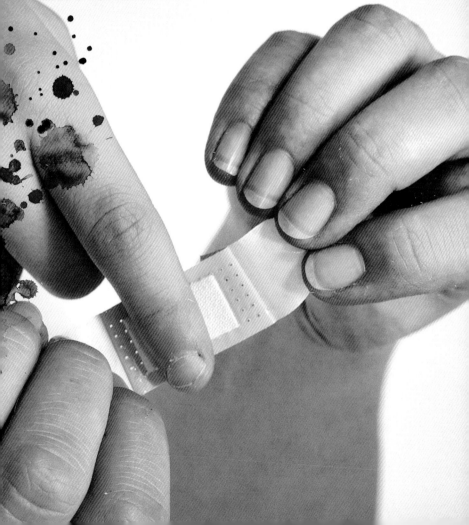

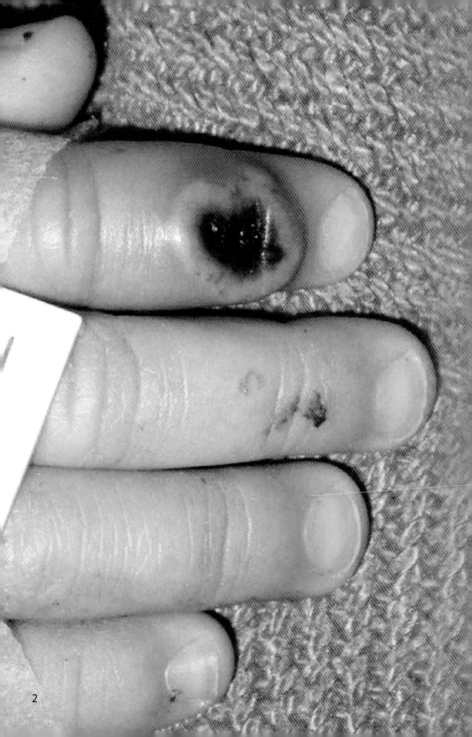

2

The Symptoms

Schyan Kautzer was really sick.

The three-year-old girl had a high fever, no appetite, and no energy. The area around the bite was covered with strange, blister-like bumps.

Mystery Illness

Schyan's worried parents rushed her to the hospital. The doctors could not figure out what was wrong with her. They ordered tests and prescribed medications. But the little girl was not getting better.

The Specialist

Then Schyan's parents mentioned that their daughter had been bitten by her pet prairie dog. The pet died not long after.

Would Schyan be next? Her doctors needed help. Fast. They called a dermatologist. That is a doctor who specializes in skin diseases.

The Question

How might the prairie dog provide a clue to Schyan's mysterious illness? What are some of the problems with keeping wild animals as pets?

Important note: Keeping any wild animal as a pet can be harmful to both people and the animals themselves. Please keep this in mind as you read this book.

Prairie dogs are native to the grasslands and prairies of North America. Their natural habitat is the best place for them to live and thrive. Living in the wild is also vital to their survival as a species.

Preview Photo

PAGE 2: **Schyan Kautzer's infected finger**

Cover design: Maria Bergós, Book&Look **Interior design:** Red Herring Design/NYC

Photo Credits ©: cover top: Marty Jo Walicki/KRT/Newscom; cover bottom: Chris and Tilde Stuart/Minden Pictures; 1: CHROMORANGE/Alexander Bernhard/Alamy Images; 2: Marshfield Clinic Health System, Inc. (MCHS). All rights reserved. Reprinted with permission from MCHS; 10: Rich Miller/The Indianapolis Star/AP Images; 12: Mike Roemer/Getty Images; 15: Marty Jo Walicki/KRT/Newscom; 16: FrankyDeMeyer/Getty Images; 19: Marshfield Clinic Health System, Inc. ("MCHS"). All rights reserved. Reprinted with permission from MCHS; 20: David De Lossy/Media Bakery; 23: Tim Vernon, LTH NHS Trust/Science Source; 25: Custom Medical Stock Photo/Alamy Images; 26 center: George Bernard/Science Source; 26 bottom: Alfredo Dagli Orti/Shutterstock; 27 center left: Steven Smith/Dreamstime; 27 bottom: Morry Gash/AP Images; 28: CDC/Getty Images; 30: CDC/Getty Images; 32: Stacie Freudenberg/AP Images; 33: CDC/James Gathany/Science Source; 34: Hazel Appleton, Health Protection Agency Centre for Infections/Science Source; 38 bottom left: Jean-Loup Charmet/Science Source; 38 bottom right: Everett Collection/Shutterstock; 40: Maryland DHMH Public Relations; 42 top: R. Maisonneuve/Science Source; 42 center: Chernetskaya/Dreamstime; 42 bottom right: Mauro Fermariello/Science Source; 43 top left: Mary Ann Liebert, Inc., publishers; 43 top right: D. Hurst/Alamy Images; 43 bottom left: Tom Schneider/imageBROKER/age fotostock; 43 bottom right: cglade/Getty Images; 44 sheep: John Foxx/Getty Images; 44 mouse: John Serrao/Science Source; 45 bubonic plague: Katerynakon/Dreamstime; 45 hantavirus: ESTIOT/age fotostock.

All other photos © Shutterstock.

A CIP catalog record of this book is available from the Library of Congress.
ISBN 978-0-531-13232-6 (library binding) 978-0-531-13297-5 (paperback)

Printed in Johor Bahru, Malaysia   108

1 2 3 4 5 6 7 8 9 10 R 30 29 28 27 26 25 24 23 22 21

PRAIRIE DOG
ALERT!

A Nasty Bite Leads to Big Trouble

CHRISTEN BROWNLEE

 SCHOLASTIC

TABLE OF CONTENTS

1

Handle with Care

A little girl and her new pets get acquainted—and sick.

On Mother's Day in 2003, three-year-old Schyan Kautzer and her parents went to a pet swap near their home in central Wisconsin. A pet swap is a place to buy and sell pets.

The Kautzer family lived on a farm. They owned lots of animals. But they always had room for more.

There was a wide variety of animals for sale at the pet swap. Some were familiar pets, like gerbils. Others—like camels and prairie dogs—are not usually kept as pets. But the Kautzer family had made a decision. If a particular animal caught their attention, they were ready to buy.

New Pets

Schyan's mother, Tammy Kautzer, had owned pet prairie dogs when she was younger. Someone at the pet swap was selling them for $95 each. The Kautzers thought the sandy-colored critters were adorable, so they bought two. Then Schyan and her parents put the prairie dogs into boxes and took them home.

THE KAUTZER FAMILY holds one of their prairie dogs.

Prairie Dog Profile

How would you like a barking squirrel as a pet?

What animal lives in a town, digs tunnels—called burrows—and barks like a dog? If you said a prairie dog, you're right! But prairie dogs aren't dogs. They're rodents. They belong to the squirrel family. Prairie dogs are burrowing squirrels, to be exact.

Prairie dogs are playful, intelligent, and very vocal. They make loud whistles and doglike barks (that's how they got their name). They also use calls to warn other prairie dogs of danger.

Prairie dogs live in colonies. Groups of prairie dog families are called *coteries*. Coteries live together in larger groups called *towns*.

13

Schyan loved playing with her new pets. But soon one of the prairie dogs started looking sick. It moped around. Its eyes were crusty. It seemed cranky, just like a sick person.

Schyan picked up the pup to put it back in its cage. It gave her finger a nasty bite. Her mother and her father, Steve Kautzer, washed the bite and kissed it.

Over the next few days, the bite mark on Schyan's finger appeared to be healing. But then the bite turned into a dark red bump. A rash of unusual-looking bumps popped up around it. And Schyan came down with a high fever.

Then the sick prairie dog died.

Schyan's parents worried that their little girl might be seriously ill. They rushed her to a nearby hospital.

SCHYAN KAUTZER shows where she was bitten by her pet prairie dog.

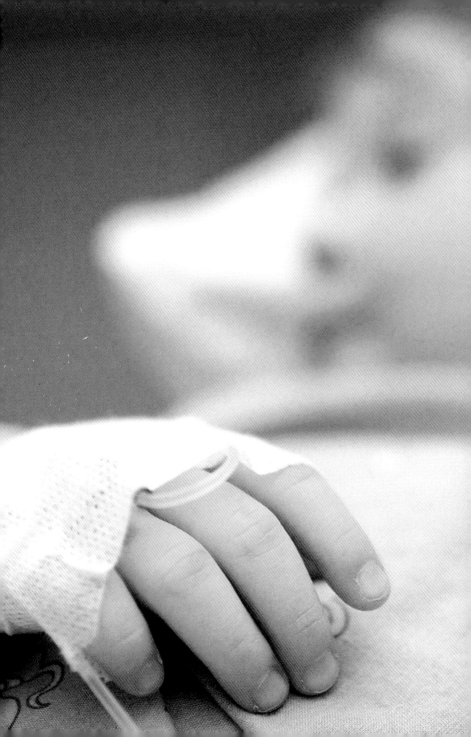

2

Call the Expert

Schyan is getting sicker. Can anyone figure out what is wrong with her?

Soon after Schyan was admitted to the hospital, Dr. Scott David arrived to talk with her parents. He said Schyan would need a few tests to help doctors diagnose her disease. He needed to know what was causing her infection before he could fight it.

The doctor took samples of Schyan's blood. Then he asked her parents a number of questions.

Had Schyan eaten or drunk anything strange? Had she been around other kids? Had anything unusual happened to her in the past few days?

Tammy Kautzer mentioned that her daughter had been nipped by a sick prairie dog. It died not long after. They had thrown the dead animal away before driving to the hospital.

The doctor told the Kautzers to dig the prairie dog's body out of the trash and bring it back to the hospital.

The prairie dog's body needed to be tested for disease. Prairie dogs are rodents, and rodents can carry many different diseases. The test results might give doctors clues about what was making Schyan sick.

Sick as a Dog

In the hospital, doctors ran test after test. But they couldn't figure out what was wrong with the young girl.

Infections like Schyan's can be caused by several types of microorganisms. Microorganisms are extremely small life-forms that can only be seen through a microscope.

One common microorganism is bacteria. There are billions of bacteria all around you. Most are harmless. But if conditions are just right, some bacteria can cause infections.

Schyan's doctors thought that her rash and fever could have been caused by a bacterial infection. So they gave her several different antibiotics. Those are drugs that attack bacteria. But the medicine didn't help, which meant that Schyan's infection probably wasn't bacterial.

Calling Dr. Melski

Schyan's doctors were perplexed. They realized they needed help. So they called Dr. John Melski, a dermatologist. That's a doctor who specializes in skin diseases. Would he be able to solve this medical mystery?

Dr. John Melski

3

Doctor Dream Team

With the help of an expert, Schyan's medical team starts to make progress.

Dr. John Melski's home phone rang on a Sunday morning. He listened as one of Schyan's doctors described the girl's symptoms. She had a high fever, loss of appetite, and fatigue. And her body was now covered with a rash of mysterious, blister-like bumps. The symptoms had appeared after Schyan was bitten by her sick prairie dog.

Schyan's illness was getting worse. "They needed my help pretty quickly," Melski says.

Searching for Clues

Melski decided to do some research before going to see Schyan in the hospital. He searched the Internet for information about diseases that prairie dogs can carry. But none of the diseases he read about caused symptoms like Schyan's.

At the hospital, Melski read the other doctors' notes about Schyan's case. He saw that antibiotics hadn't eased her symptoms. She still had a rash and a fever.

"I realized that this was a strange case," Melski says. "Most of the diseases I uncovered [in my research] should have been treated by the antibiotics, but Schyan wasn't getting better."

When Melski examined the bumps on the girl's hands, he got his first clue about the disease. The bumps were full of fluid. Some of them had dimples in the center.

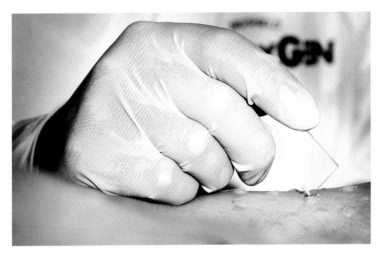

A DOCTOR TAKES a sample of the fluid inside the bumps on a patient's skin. The sample will be tested to find out what is causing the infection.

Going Viral

Melski realized that these bumps could be symptoms of an infection caused by a virus. Viruses are a type of very tiny germs. Unlike bacteria, viruses can't be killed by antibiotics.

Some viral infections, such as chicken pox or cold sores, cause bumps that look similar to the sores on Schyan's body. "My instincts told me that what I was seeing was viral," Melski says.

Melski knew that the fluid inside the bumps held more clues. He put on sterile gloves and cut open one of the blisters. He drained the fluid onto a glass slide. Then he added a stain that sticks to viruses to make them easier to see under a microscope. But Melski saw nothing.

Skin Sample

Hunting down the virus would take more drastic measures. Melski needed to do a biopsy. In a biopsy, a doctor removes a sample of human tissue, such as a slice of skin. Then the sample is examined under a microscope.

Melski numbed the skin on Schyan's hand. Then he cut out a bump the size of a pencil eraser. He sent the tissue sample to the hospital's laboratory.

In the lab, technicians cut the sample into thin slices and put them on glass slides. Dr. Kurt Reed, a pathologist, looked at the slides. Pathologists are trained to examine tissue samples for signs of disease. Reed told Melski that he'd been right. Schyan had a virus.

A MEDICAL TECHNICIAN looks at a thin slice of tissue on a slide.

Critter Carriers

Here are some milestones in the history of zoonotic diseases. (That is what you call diseases that are transmitted to humans by other animals.)

1918: Global Disaster There was worldwide panic as the Spanish flu—a strain of the H1N1 virus—sped around the world. H1N1 commonly occurs in pigs. But this outbreak killed close to 50 million people.

1347–1351 **1885** **1918**

1347–1351: Rats Carry Plague In October 1347, a ship docked in Messina, Italy. It was carrying rats that would spread a disease that is now known as the bubonic plague. This bacterial infection killed one-third of the people in Europe.

1885: First Rabies Survivor In France, nine-year-old Joseph Meister was bitten by a dog that was sick with the rabies virus. Back then, rabies had always been fatal. But scientist Louis Pasteur (above) saved the boy by giving him the first vaccine for rabies. The vaccine was a weakened form of the virus. It made the boy's body produce antibodies that fought the virus.

1986: Mysterious Mad Cows
English farmers noticed that some of their cows were acting, well, crazy. The cows were nervous and staggering. Scientists discovered they had a new illness. It was nicknamed "mad cow disease." Some people who ate meat from these cows would also be killed by a similar disease.

2019: A Global Pandemic Starts A respiratory disease named COVID-19 caused by a new coronavirus is first identified in the city of Wuhan in China. It is believed the virus came from a live-animal market and "jumped" to human beings. The aggressive and deadly illness quickly made its way to every corner of the world and turned into a pandemic with global effects.

1963: Germ Fighters Unite A group of scientists and doctors formed the Infectious Diseases Society of America. Today the society works to help diagnose, prevent, and treat zoonotic and other contagious diseases.

1963   1986 1993   2004 2019

1993: Southwestern Outbreak
About 40 people in the southwestern U.S. came down with similar symptoms. They were coughing, wheezing, and couldn't breathe. About half of them died. Scientists discovered that they were sick with a hantavirus, a flulike disease that's spread by rodents.

2004: Rabies Breakthrough In Wisconsin, 15-year-old Jeanna Giese was bitten by a bat. She developed symptoms of the rabies disease. For the rabies vaccine to work, it must be given before these symptoms appear. But Jeanna's doctor put her in a coma so the virus couldn't attack her brain. A week later, she started to recover. She was the first person to survive rabies without having had the rabies vaccine.

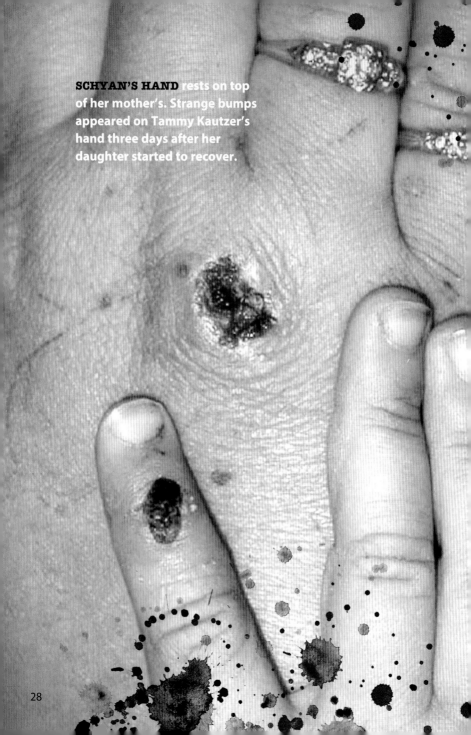

SCHYAN'S HAND rests on top of her mother's. Strange bumps appeared on Tammy Kautzer's hand three days after her daughter started to recover.

4

Outbreak!

Schyan starts to recover. But a new patient gets sick with the same symptoms.

Doctors now knew that Schyan's illness was caused by a viral infection. But they still had to figure out what type of virus she had. In the meantime, they made sure she got enough nutrients and fluids. Schyan slowly began to recover as her immune system fought off the virus.

After three days in the hospital, Schyan felt much better. Her fever was gone. Her appetite was back. She was more energetic.

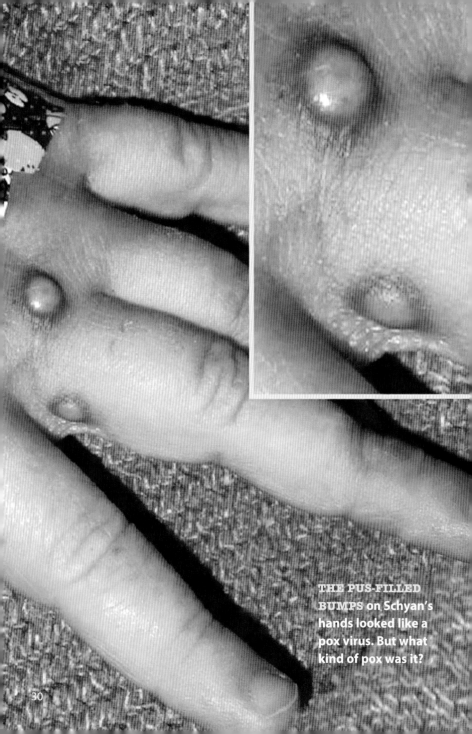

THE PUS-FILLED BUMPS on Schyan's hands looked like a pox virus. But what kind of pox was it?

A New Patient

But now Schyan's mother was sick. Blister-like bumps were forming around a cut on Tammy Kautzer's hand. She also had a fever.

Dr. Melski took a skin sample from Tammy. Pictures were taken of the bumps on her skin so Melski could show her symptoms to other doctors.

Melski shared the images with Dr. Reed. They were almost certain that the pictures showed a pox infection. Pox viruses cause raised, infected bumps.

Still, there are many different types of pox viruses. How could the doctors figure out which virus this was?

Mystery Pox

Over the next few days, other cases of the strange pox popped up in Wisconsin, Illinois, and Indiana. These patients had also come into contact with prairie dogs.

It was time to call the Centers for Disease Control and Prevention (CDC). This government organization is in charge of protecting public health. It works to track and control the spread of contagious diseases.

Melski and other doctors working with the pox patients met with officials from the CDC. The officials told the doctors to post pictures of the mystery pox virus on the Internet. That way, doctors around the world could share their knowledge.

Within days, test results confirmed a diagnosis. Schyan and Tammy Kautzer had a virus called monkeypox.

REBECCA McLESTER was one of dozens of people in the Midwest who got monkey-pox from pet prairie dogs in 2003. Here she is playing with her favor-ite Neapolitan mastiff puppy, Miracle, outside her home.

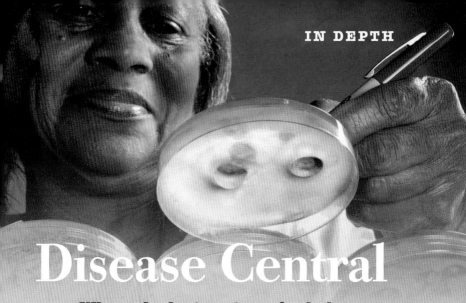

Disease Central

Where do doctors turn for help solving medical mysteries? The CDC is a good place to start.

What is the CDC? The Centers for Disease Control and Prevention (CDC) is an agency of the U.S. government. It was founded in 1946 as the Communicable Disease Center.

Where is it? Its headquarters and main laboratories are in Atlanta, Georgia.

What does it do? The CDC works to protect public health by informing the public about infectious diseases. Some divisions conduct disease research, prevention, control, and education programs. Others help train doctors, provide public health information, and work with state and local agencies on immunization programs.

What can the CDC teach me? The CDC has a great website: www.cdc.gov. It's loaded with information about interesting diseases. It also has tips on how to have a healthy lifestyle and how to prepare for emergencies. You'll even find stories from people who survived a worldwide outbreak of flu in 1918!

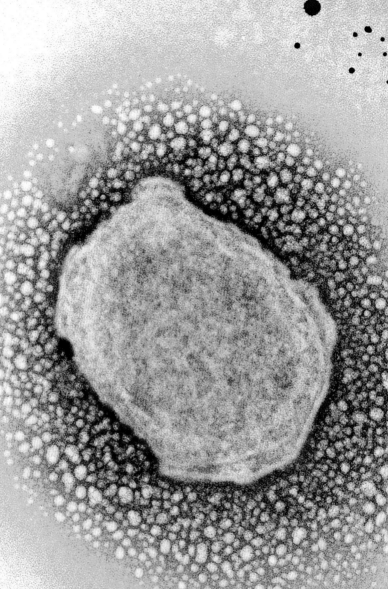

A POWERFUL MICROSCOPE is needed to see a tiny virus. This is what monkeypox looks like under an electron microscope. This microscope uses a beam of electrons instead of light to magnify objects.

5

Monkey Trouble

How did a virus from Africa infect a prairie dog in Wisconsin?

Monkeypox! The diagnosis was a surprise. Monkeypox is a rare zoonotic disease. *Zoonotic* describes diseases that animals can pass to humans. Monkeypox was first seen in lab monkeys in about 1958. About 12 years later, it showed up in humans.

Monkeypox had never been seen in the United States before. It is most common in central and western Africa.

So how had it traveled to the U.S.? Scientists

from the CDC investigated animals that had come into contact with the infected prairie dogs. They learned that the Kautzers' pups had been kept next to a Gambian giant rat.

That was it! Gambian rats live in several African countries and can be carriers of monkeypox. The rats can look healthy but make other animals sick. That's what had happened to the Kautzers' prairie dog.

In total, 92 people in six midwestern states got monkeypox infections from imported rodents. That included Schyan and her mother and father. All the patients survived. Dr. Melski says that giving these patients the right care was key to their

GAMBIAN GIANT RATS can carry monkeypox and spread it to humans and other animals.

recovery. People can die from monkeypox if they don't get medical care.

On the Lookout

Once the doctors figured out what disease had struck Schyan, they were able to treat the other patients.

Schyan and her family have made a full recovery. Melski and other doctors now know what to look for if there's ever another monkeypox outbreak.

Monkeypox isn't a typical disease carried by prairie dogs, says Melski. "That's why I missed it in my initial research." He adds, "Next time, we'll be more prepared." **X**

Pick a Pox

Poxes have been plaguing people for thousands of years. Here are some of the more infamous ones.

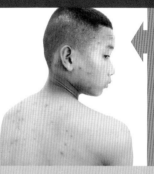

Chicken pox usually causes only a mild illness in children. That's good because it is highly contagious. Symptoms include fever, fatigue, and small, blister-like bumps that can be very itchy. Today, there is a vaccine for chicken pox.

Smallpox was once a widespread disease. Thanks to worldwide vaccination programs, it was finally wiped out in 1979. Symptoms of this dreaded disease began with a fever and body aches. Then a rash of blisters spread all over the person's body. About a third of the people who got smallpox died. Those who survived often suffered from severe scarring.

Cowpox is related to smallpox but usually affects cows. In humans, it's like a milder version of smallpox. The first vaccines against smallpox came from cowpox. In 1796, Dr. Edward Jenner injected pus from a cowpox blister into a young boy's arm. The boy developed a mild case of cowpox. Then Jenner infected the boy with smallpox, but the boy did not get sick. Jenner's experiment was a success! His work saved many lives.

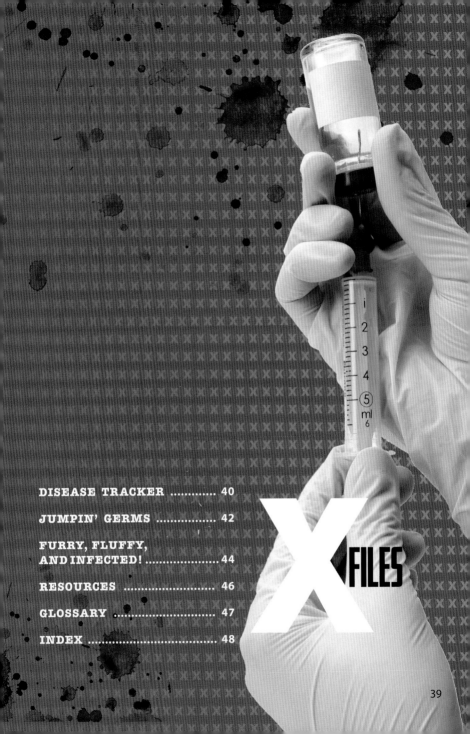

XFILES

Disease Tracker

Epidemiologist Kim Mitchell specializes in zoonotic diseases.

How did you get into your field?
MITCHELL: I stumbled into the study of epidemiology as I was finishing up my undergraduate degree. [Epidemiologists study epidemics. Those are outbreaks of diseases that affect large groups of people.] I hadn't even heard of epidemiology at the time, but I started reading about it and was intrigued. I ended up applying to public health school instead of medical school like I planned.

KIM MITCHELL is an epidemiologist for the Maryland Department of Health and Mental Hygiene.

When you're at a dinner party, how do you explain your job?
MITCHELL: My exact title is Chief of Rabies and Vector-Borne Diseases. What this means is that I monitor and track diseases like rabies and West Nile virus in animals and humans. They call what I do disease surveillance.

What's the hardest part of your job?
MITCHELL: The biggest challenge is getting by with limited resources. Like many government agencies, we have a tight budget and are often short-staffed. Sometimes we have to get creative to get things done.

What do you like most about what you do?
MITCHELL: I like knowing that I am helping the larger community. My efforts contribute to the overall health and safety of all Marylanders.

What was your most memorable case?
MITCHELL: It's hard to pick. I would say the most fascinating cases involve [people] getting bitten by monkeys while traveling overseas. In these cases, the challenge is often determining the kind of monkey, the nature of the exposure, and the type of treatment the person may have already gotten.

Jumpin' Germs

Here are a zoonotic disease researcher's tools of the trade.

IN THE LAB

1 Petri dishes and test tubes

Doctors and scientists take samples from a patient's body. They use these samples to grow bacteria and viruses in petri dishes and test tubes. What's the point? Taking a close look at these germs allows scientists to identify and study them.

2 Tissue sectioner
Like a meat slicer at a deli, this machine cuts tissue samples taken from biopsies into thin slices. Scientists can examine these slices for the presence of harmful bacteria or viruses.

3 Transmission electron microscope

This high-powered microscope uses electrons to view objects that can't be seen with the naked eye.

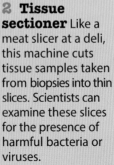

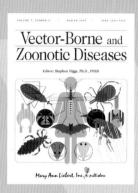

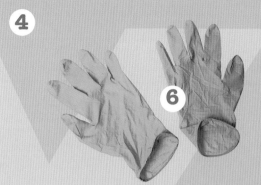

RESEARCH AND REFERENCE

4 Journals
Scientists read scientific and professional publications to keep up with the latest research on zoonotic diseases.

5 Internet
The Internet is a great resource for medical researchers. They can share information with other scientists, research unfamiliar symptoms, and identify rare germs.

SAFETY EQUIPMENT

6 Gloves People who study zoonotic diseases often wear gloves to protect themselves from germs. Gloves also keep lab technicians' hands free from dyes and other chemicals.

7 Lab coat
Lab technicians wear lab coats to protect their clothing from hazardous materials. The coats are often white, which makes it easy to spot spills and splashes.

8 Goggles
These protect scientists' eyes from germs, stains, and harmful liquids used in the lab.

Furry, Fluffy, and Infected!

Before you pat that pet, check out the disease-causing germs that some animals can pass on to humans!

Disease	Common Host	
Toxoplasmosis	Cat	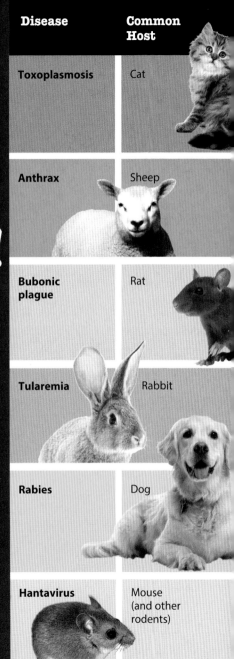
Anthrax	Sheep	
Bubonic plague	Rat	
Tularemia	Rabbit	
Rabies	Dog	
Hantavirus	Mouse (and other rodents)	

Toxoplasma gondii	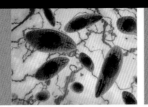	Muscle aches and pains, fatigue, swollen glands
Bacillus anthracis		High fever, cough, sore throat, headache, nausea, death. Cows and other grazing animals can also become infected with anthrax.
Yersinia pestis	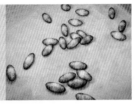	Chills, fever, diarrhea, swollen glands, headaches, death. Rats and humans contract the bubonic plague when they are bitten by infected fleas.
Francisella tularensis	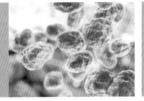	Fever, headache, cough, diarrhea
Rhabdovirus	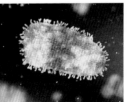	Anxiety, muscle spasms and weakness, drooling, death. Rabies can also be carried by animals such as raccoons, cats, and ferrets.
Hantavirus	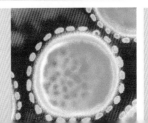	Fever, trouble breathing, heart failure

RESOURCES

Here's a selection of books for more information about zoonotic and other infectious diseases.

NONFICTION

Biskup, Agnieszka Jòzefina. *Understanding Viruses with Max Axiom, Super Scientist: 4D An Augmented Reading Science Experience (Graphic Science 4D).* North Mankato, Minnesota: Capstone, 2019.

DiConsiglio, John. *When Birds Get Flu and Cows Go Mad!: How Safe Are We? (24/7: Science Behind the Scenes: Medical Files).* New York: Scholastic, 2007.

Friedlander, Mark P., Jr. *Outbreak: Disease Detectives at Work (Discovery!).* Minneapolis: Twenty-First Century Books, 2009.

Hall, Linley Erin. *Killer Viruses (Doomsday Scenarios: Separating Fact from Fiction).* New York: Rosen, 2010.

Jarrow, Gail. *Bubonic Panic: When Plague Invaded America.* Honesdale, Pennsylvania: Calkins Creek, 2016.

Rooney, Anne. *You Wouldn't Want to Live Without Vaccinations!* New York: Scholastic, 2015.

Woolf, Alex. *The Science of Acne and Warts: The Itchy Truth About Skin (The Science of the Body).* New York: Scholastic, 2018.

FICTION

Cooney, Caroline B. *Code Orange.* New York: Delacorte Press, 2005.

Danziger, Paula. *You Can't Eat Your Chicken Pox, Amber Brown.* New York: Puffin Books, 2006.

Hirsch, Jeff. *The Eleventh Plague.* New York: Scholastic, 2012.

Reichs, Kathy. *Virals.* New York: Puffin Books, 2011.

Scarrow, Alex. *Plague Land: No Escape.* Chicago: Sourcebooks Fire, 2019.

Williams, Mark London. *City of Ruins (Danger Boy).* Somerville, Massachusetts: Candlewick, 2007.

Williams, Sarah DeFord. *Palace Beautiful.* New York: Puffin Books, 2011.

GLOSSARY

bacteria (bak-TIHR-ee-uh) *noun* single-celled life-forms that can cause disease in humans and other animals

carrier (KA-ree-ur) *noun* a human or other animal that carries a contagious disease and can pass it on to others without getting sick

contagious (kon-TAY-juss) *adjective* describing a disease that is transmitted from one living thing to another

diagnose (dye-uhg-NOHSS) *verb* to identify a disease or illness

fatal (FAY-tul) *adjective* causing death

fatigue (fuh-TEEG) *noun* extreme tiredness

immune system (ih-MYOON SIS-tuhm) *noun* the network of defenses that protects the body against disease and infection

infection (in-FEK-shun) *noun* the uncontrolled growth of germs in a living thing

monkeypox (MUHNG-kee-pocks) *noun* a viral disease that causes fever, fatigue, and raised bumps on the skin

pox (POCKS) *noun* any of several viral diseases that produce pus-filled pimples that leave scars on the skin

pus (PUHSS) *noun* a thick, yellow liquid produced in infected tissue; it is made of dead white blood cells, germs, and tissue cells

rodent (ROHD-uhnt) *noun* a mammal with large, sharp front teeth that are used for gnawing; common rodents are rats, chipmunks, mice, squirrels, and prairie dogs

sterile (STER-uhl) *adjective* free of any bacteria or viruses

tissue (TISH-oo) *noun* a mass of similar cells that form a particular part of an organ of a plant or animal

vaccine (vak-SEEN) *noun* a medicine that prepares the body to fight off a germ

virus (VYE-ruhss) *noun* a tiny germ, smaller than bacteria, that grows and reproduces in living cells

zoonotic (zoh-uh-NOT-ik) *adjective* having to do with a disease that is transmitted to humans by other animals

INDEX